Baby's Christmas

By Esther Wilkin

Illustrated by Eloise Wilkin

A GOLDEN BOOK · NEW YORK

Text copyright © 1959, renewed 1987 by Penguin Random House LLC.
All rights reserved. Published in the United States by Golden Books, an imprint of Random House
Children's Books, a division of Penguin Random House LLC, 1745 Broadway, New York, NY
10019, and in Canada by Penguin Random House Canada Limited, Toronto. Originally published
by Golden Press, New York, in 1959. Golden Books, A Golden Book, A Little Golden Book,
the G colophon, and the distinctive spine design are registered trademarks of Penguin Random
House LLC. A Little Golden Book Classic is a trademark of Penguin Random House LLC.
randomhousekids.com
Educators and librarians, for a variety of teaching tools, visit us at
RHTeachersLibrarians.com
Library of Congress Control Number: 2016954052
ISBN 978-1-5247-2051-3 (trade) – ISBN 978-1-5247-2052-0 (ebook)
Printed in the United States of America
10 9 8 7 6 5 4 3 2 1

What did Santa leave for Baby?

Let's go in
and see.

Here is Baby's Christmas tree,
With the gingerbread boys and the candy canes,
The twinkly lights and the colored balls,
Green and yellow, red and blue.
Find the Star at the top of the tree,
Shining bright for all to see.
Find baby Jesus asleep in the hay,
For He was born on Christmas Day.

Santa left a music box that plays a little tune:
Rock-a-bye, baby, on the tree top!
When the wind blows the cradle will rock,
When the bough breaks the cradle will fall.
Down will come baby, cradle and all.

He left a string of wooden beads,
Pink and blue and white.

Santa left a teddy bear,

A dog with floppy ears,

A little drum to beat upon,

A kiddie car that steers.

Santa left a rubber ball
To roll along the floor,

A picture book,

A kitty cat,

And more, more, more!

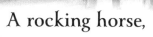

A rocking horse,

A bouncy seat,

A shovel
and a pail,

A rubber duck,
  a little boat
For Baby dear to sail.

Santa left some
building blocks,

A milk truck,

And a train,

A little cart to pull around
The room and back again.

Where will Baby keep the toys,
All piled up to the skies?

Just turn the page and you will see
A great big, BIG SURPRISE!

For Santa left a toy box,
A red and yellow toy box,
So pretty and so gay!

And that's where Baby puts the toys,
At the end of every day!